FRANCIS FR
PRIVATE E

Sam McBratney
and Kim Blundell

Collins

COLOUR JETS

Dad on the Run	Sarah Garland
Stinker Muggles and the Dazzle Bug	Elizabeth Laird
Francis Fry, Private Eye	Sam McBratney
Even Stevens F.C.	Michael Rosen

First published in Great Britain by
HarperCollins Publishers Ltd 1995

9 8 7 6 5

Text © Sam McBratney 1995
Illustrations © Kim Blundell 1995

The author and illustrator assert the moral right to be identified as the author and illustrator of the work.

A CIP record for this title is available
from the British Library.

ISBN 0 00 675027-3

Printed and bound in Italy

Chapter 1

Hi.

Fry is the name – Francis Fry. I'm a Private Eye. It's hard to spot me in this picture because the good detective never stands out in a crowd.

Think about it.

This is my office.

I like a swivel chair.
Turning round in circles helps me think.

What sort of work do I do?

Well, I find things.

Sometimes it's missing people.

Sometimes it's missing jewellery.

Only this morning a man walked into my office…

I told him my fees. I don't come
cheap, but he didn't faint.

I looked at the mug shot and spun round twice in my swivel chair. Jacko was red, green and yellow and a few other shades thrown in.

Please, Mr Fry. He's so intelligent. He knows when Neighbours comes on.

For a fee I'll look for a needle in a haystack.

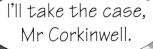

I'll take the case, Mr Corkinwell.

Chapter 2

First I had to have some lunch.
I bought a newspaper and nipped into
a burger joint for a cheese quarterpounder with double fried onions and
Thousand Island dressing.

THEFT FROM LOCAL HOUSE

SIX PARROTS STOLEN
IN NIGHT-TIME RAID

More stolen parrots!
Well, eating a cheese quarterpounder
gives you time to think.

I've known people to steal paper clips, manhole covers, plastic gnomes, and even wet cement in buckets – but parrots?

Was this a lonely thief – did he want someone to talk to?

Or maybe a parrot had bitten off his finger in childhood and he was now seeking revenge.

Or was there big money in parrots?

Speaking of money, I heard a Mr Higginbottom on local radio as I drove out to the Corkinwell house.

Mr Higginbottom, an expert in tropical animals with the RSPCA, had just won two million pounds on the pools.

I made a note of the name.
An expert in tropical animals
might come in handy in
this case.

Chapter 3

At the Corkinwell house I spotted a little pile of dark powder in Jacko's empty cage.

Soot!

Mr Corkinwell, have you had your chimney swept recently?

Why, ye

And have you the name of the sweep, Mr Corkinwell?

Yes, I got his name from a friend at the jumble sale. Funnily enough, she lost her parrot too, you know.

Another missing parrot.

Same sweep.

Think about it.

Chapter 4

Inside half an hour I was rapping on
the front door of

TONY ANGELONI
CHIMNEY SWEEP TO
THE ARISTOCRACY

My plan was simple. Tell him I needed
my chimney swept and tell him I had a
parrot. Get him round to my place and
catch him red-handed. The best plans
are always simple.

He invited me in.
There was a dog on the carpet
watching television.

Your parrot?

I told him that my chimney smoked like… um… a chimney and I didn't think it was good for the parrot.

I don't want Horace getting a smoker's cough.

Even the dog looked at me strangely. Maybe I was overdoing it. But Angeloni seemed to take the bait.

He went into the hall muttering
something about making a phone call.

Within seconds the police arrived!

Frankie Fry, I thought, this feels like trouble.

Chapter 5

Luckily I knew the Chief Inspector.

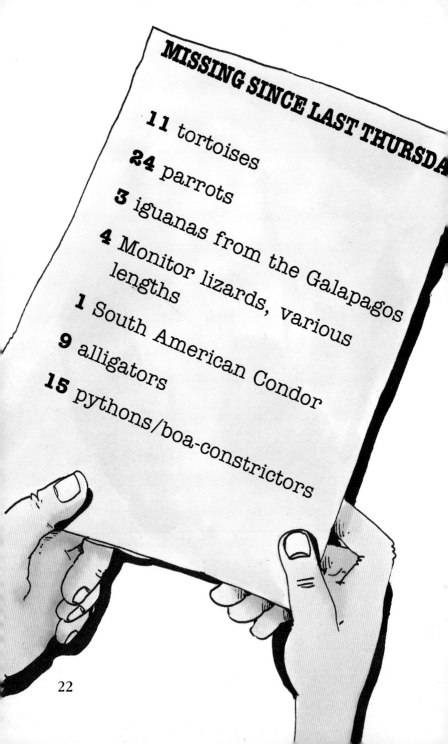

Jumping jackdaws!
It was like a Who's Who from the zoo.

"Stolen," said Charlie, "by a smooth thief posing as a vet, a window-cleaner and a sweep. It seems that nobody's fancy pet is safe any more."

I ate some liquorice, which I consider to be an important brain food.

I left with the list of missing
beasts in my pocket.
Iguanas, lizards, tortoises
and snakes. Stone the crows!

Not to mention alligators.
I reached for the car phone.
When you're in trouble,
dial an expert.
It sometimes helps.

Mr Higginbottom of the RSPCA agreed
to see me at once.

26

"Oh yes," replied Mr Higginbottom. "They make very good shoes and handbags, after all. A good South American parrot will easily fetch £500."

He suggested I put an ad in the paper:
WANTED – BRAZILIAN PARROT, that
sort of thing.

The thief will contact you if he's looking for a quick sale.

Not a bad idea, I thought.
Flush him into the open.

It wouldn't half change me,
I thought.

Chapter 6

My ad appeared in the local paper that afternoon.

PARROTS, LIZARDS AND ALLIGATORS WANTED.
BEST PRICES YOU'LL FIND.

Two people called me next morning – a man with a baby alligator and a woman with a vulture for sale. I wrote down their names and addresses on a piece of paper.

Then my door opened…
What an oddball! He had one of those
monster moustaches that make you
look as if you've just had your mouth
thatched.

31

I looked at the bird on his wrist.
"That's a pigeon," I said.

He held the bird up
to the light.

Is it?

"Parrots come from the jungle,"
I remarked. "*That* comes from Trafalgar
Square."

The man smiled at me with bright intelligent eyes, and I had the strangest feeling that I'd seen him somewhere before.

He hadn't gone long when it
hit me! How did he get my address?
My ad had only given a telephone number.

Then I looked at my desk. The piece of
paper had gone. He'd swiped the names of
my two callers!

Even now he could be heading off to
steal that lady's vulture, the swine.

I sat down in my swivel chair.
While turning anti-clockwise I noticed
the card he'd dropped.

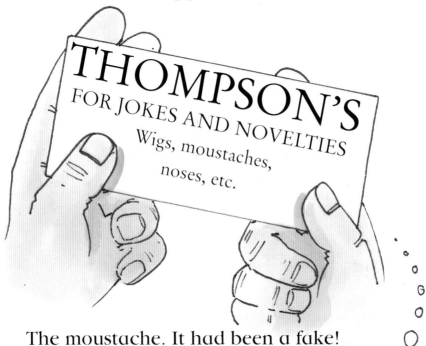

THOMPSON'S
FOR JOKES AND NOVELTIES
Wigs, moustaches,
noses, etc.

The moustache. It had been a fake!

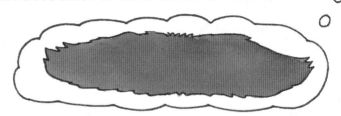

Chapter 7

In less than a minute I was at Thompson's Joke Shop.

The man who bought the moustache! What did he look like?

Like anybody else, really. Except Tom Cruise. I'd have noticed if he'd looked like Tom Cruise.

"Bald?" I said. "Short, tall, fat? A scar?
Old, shifty, foreign?"

Maybe...

She wouldn't have noticed
an alien!

If it's any help,
he drove a two-tone yellow
Mercedes convertible with
beige interior trim, fitted
stereo, central locking and
matching hub caps.

FALSE
NOSES
PICK
ONE!

Chapter 8

I got a nasty shock later that day.
I had half a second to duck the
handbag-shaped missile.

Man, this was awkward. I did my best to
explain what I thought had happened.

x

x

She wasn't impressed.

Burgled?
I wasn't burgled. He asked if he
could take my vulture out to his car.
He said his cat was in the car and he
wanted to see if the cat was allergic
to the vulture. Or vice versa.

There's a fool born every minute.
I mean, he just drove away with the
vulture!

"Ordinary," she wailed. "And I gave that stinker tea. 'I'll have a _jot_ of milk and a _tittle_ of sugar,' he said."

I hope my Agatha bites the nose off his FACE!

I hoped so too.

Then I locked the door in case the geezer with no alligator showed up.

I ate some liquorice, spun round in my chair and played some heavy metal. It sometimes helps.

Who is this thief?
Where is he keeping the stolen creatures?
Where is he now?

Probably parked somewhere, laughing his leg off at me in his yellow Mercedes, I thought.

It was time, I decided, for a cup of tea –
with a little jot of milk and more than a
tittle of sugar.

I whipped off my headphones. The vulture-snatcher had used those unusual words, but I'd also heard them before...

Lights were flashing in my head, pennies were dropping. Had I hit the jackpot?

The bright, intelligent eyes.

The tramp.

The knowledge of animals.

The new Mercedes.

HIGGINBOTTOM!

46

Chapter 9

I swallowed my liquorice.

Can I speak to Mr Higginbottom, please?

Sorry, Mr Higginbottom starts his world cruise today.

The yacht! I snatched up my car keys and hit the street running.

Was I already too late?

No. The yacht was easy to find.
It was the one with the yellow
Mercedes parked beside it.

I picked up a crate and walked on board as if I was one of the crew.

On board the yacht I could not believe my own eyes. I saw a sand pit crawling with tortoises; glass containers of lizards; a vulture with wings the colour of midnight blue. And parrots!

Was this Noah's Ark?

Higginbottom stood with his back to me, admiring the coils of a mighty python.

"Where are the alligators, Higginbottom?" I said. "Down below? Or sold already?"

I saw again the look of horror that comes over every criminal's face when the good guys catch up.

Why Mr Fry!

"The very same," I said. "And don't try anything funny – I'm an expert kick-boxer. You wouldn't stand a chance."

"I'm sure I wouldn't," he sighed.
"Oh well, it was fun while it lasted.
Some fresh tea...?"

Why not? With a _jot_ of milk and a _tittle_ of sugar.

Well, I cannot describe all the thoughts that swam through my muddy old brain once I'd taken a sip of Higginbottom's tea. The last thought I had was:

I didn't even remember conking out and crumbling in a heap on the floor.

Then I saw my reflection.

Jumping jackdaws! I didn't know the face in the beard looking back at me.

I know your rotten racket, Higginbottom. You steal pets and sell them for a quick buck. What kind of a skunk are you, anyway?

He tickled a parrot under its beak.

"This is Henry," he told me. "Henry is a parrot. Henry the parrot has lived in the same dark room off the Edgware Road for fifteen years, watching the same Swiss cheese plant creeping slowly up the same greasy walls."

"What are you getting at, Higginbottom?" I asked.

"I mean that if I was a parrot, I'd like to feel the warm and tropical rains trickling off my feathers," he replied.

Tell me — if you were Francis Fry the parrot, which would you prefer? A room off the Edgware Road? Or here — in the Amazon jungle?

Jeepers. The Amazon jungle.
I could have done with a stick of
liquorice right now.

Higginbottom gently removed Henry
from the cage and tried to make him fly.

"He doesn't want to go," he said.
"He's been in prison too long.
Come on, Henry – *fly.*"

Higginbottom flung the old bird into
the air.

I took a couple of deep breaths. This sometimes helps.

"As a bird, Mr Fry," said Higginbottom with a crafty smile. "As free as a bird."

Old Henry let out a squawk, possibly of joy, and made a bolt for the Amazon jungle.

Chapter 11

Three days later I did a bit of flying myself. Higginbottom put me on a plane and sent me home.

I phoned Charlie, the Chief Inspector, and told him the whole story.

"We'll get that thieving swine some day," he snarled down the phone.

Personally, I didn't think we'd ever see Higginbottom again.

Try and see it from the parrot's point of view, Charlie.

It sometimes helps.